Barbie™

50+ Fantastic Recipes from Barbie & Her Friends

weldon**owen**

Contents

Let's Cook!

Hey, friends! I try to make every day a good day in every possible way. That includes doing my best at school, getting some exercise, playing with my pets, and hanging out with my family and friends! One of the best ways I know of to make every day as great as it can be is to eat healthy food, and one of the best ways to be sure I do that is to cook it myself (with some help when I need it, of course).

Cooking your own food isn't just good for you—it's creative and fun and delicious! These are some of my favorite recipes, and I know they'll become some of your favorites too. Whether you're a beginner in the kitchen or have some cooking experience, you will find something here you enjoy, and for every meal and occasion.

Start with a simple recipe, such as Berry & Yogurt Parfait (page 21), and work your way up to something more challenging that will be super satisfying to conquer, such as Chicken & Coconut Curry (page 84) or Chewy Chocolate Meringues (page 113). And get your friends involved (with an adult helper's permission!). Make cooking an activity at your next slumber party. Whip up a fun and healthy snack such as Crispy Chickpeas (page 51) for movie-watching and Cinnamon-Spiced Buttermilk Waffles (page 16) for breakfast the next morning.

Cooking isn't just a fun activity, though—it's a way of life!

— Barbie

Barbie's Best Cooking Tips

STAY ORGANIZED

Be prepared! First, read through the recipe from beginning to end. Then, gather the equipment and ingredients you'll need and lay them on a clean work surface. Next, prepare any ingredients you can in advance. As you work, always keep your hands and the area clean. As soon as you're done with an ingredient, put it away; when you've finished using a tool, set it aside for washing. And don't forget to set a timer to be sure you are cooking or baking the recipe for the right amount of time!

PRACTICE KITCHEN SAFETY

If you're comfortable using a knife, ask an adult to help you choose the correct type for the task, and then hold it firmly by the handle as you work. When you're not using the knife, place it somewhere safe so it won't fall onto the floor or be grabbed by a younger sibling. If you're working with an electric appliance, keep it unplugged except when in use. To guard against burns, never touch a hot oven or a hot pan without first putting on an oven mitt. When you take a lid off of a saucepan or casserole dish that has been on the stove or in the oven, tip it away from you to avoid getting burned with steam. And don't forget to give your freshly prepared food time to cool just a little bit before sampling it!

PRACTICE FOOD SAFETY

Being a safe cook is about more than knowing how to handle a knife—you need to know how to handle food safely too! Only cook with fresh ingredients. If something smells funny or is past the expiration date, throw it away. Wash all of your fruits and veggies in cool water before cooking or eating them; always clean your cutting boards with hot soapy water right after you use them with raw chicken, meat, or fish; and always wash your hands before you begin cooking and after you've handled raw chicken, meat, or fish. Last of all, keep cold foods cold. Always thaw frozen ingredients in the refrigerator, not on the countertop. And if you have leftovers, cover them tightly and refrigerate them as soon as you're done eating! (Some baked goods can be stored at room temperature.)

ASK FOR HELP IF NEEDED

Always have an adult helper nearby when you are cooking. Cooking requires working with knives, hot stovetops and ovens, and electric appliances—all of which can be a little bit tricky if you don't have a lot of experience with it. It's not only ok to ask for help—even if what you are doing doesn't involve any of those things—you absolutely should! Safety comes first, before anything else. Look for the helping hand (shown above) on recipes that might require some assistance.

Kitchen Tools & Equipment

Having the right tools makes cooking easier and more fun, and helps guarantee that your recipes will turn out great every time. This is a good basic list of things you'll need to make the recipes in this book. Go through them with an adult helper who can explain what the items are and how to safely use each one. Don't be afraid to ask questions!

Sharp knife	Blender	Vegetable peeler
Cutting board	Kitchen scissors	Box grater
Colander	Rubber spatula	Muffin pan
Strainer	Liquid measuring cups	Rimmed baking sheet
Saucepans	Dry measuring cups	Metal spatula
Skillet/frying pan	Measuring spoons	Tongs
Baking dish	Can opener	Rolling pin
Stand mixer	Wire cooling rack	Wooden spoon
Hand-held mixer	Wire whisk	Cookie cutters

Essential Skills

Making sure your recipe turns out just right starts at the very beginning of making it. Knowing a few terms and techniques will set you on the road to success every time you cook!

KNOW THE LINGO

BAKE: To cook food in the oven.

BEAT: Using a spoon or whisk to combine ingredients and make a smooth mixture, or to whip air into them to make them lighter. A good example is beating raw eggs.

BOIL: Heating liquid such as broth or water in a pan over high heat on the stove until big bubbles come to the surface and then break.

BROWN: To cook something on the stove or in the oven until it starts to turn brown on the outside. You can brown both chicken and cookies!

CHILL: Placing an ingredient or a prepared dish in the refrigerator to keep it fresh and safe to eat, as well as to make it cool or cold.

CHOP: Using a sharp knife (be sure an adult helper is close by!) and a cutting board to break down an ingredient into small pieces so it will cook faster and blend more easily with other ingredients. Always try to make sure all the pieces are about the same size so they cook evenly.

COMBINE: Using a spoon, whisk, or spatula to mix ingredients together.

DRAIN: Pouring something through a colander to get rid of the liquid and separate it from any solid ingredients. When pasta is done cooking, you pour it with the cooking water through a colander set in the sink so you can toss it with sauce!

GRATE: Running an ingredient such as cheese across the large holes of a grater to make smaller pieces.

GREASE: Rubbing oil or butter in a baking pan or dish—or spraying it with cooking spray—to keep foods from sticking when they are baked or cooked.

MIX: Using a spoon, whisk, or spatula to blend ingredients together.

PEEL: Removing the tough outside of a vegetable or fruit with a vegetable peeler.

SHRED: Running an ingredient such as cheese across a grater to make long, thin strips.

SIMMER: Cooking something at low heat so that it just barely bubbles. Soups and cooked sauces are simmered. To simmer something, first cook it over high heat until it starts to boil, then turn down the heat.

SLICE: Using a sharp knife (be sure an adult helper is close by!) and a cutting board to create thin pieces of something—such as a carrot, cucumber, or potato. Always try to make sure all the pieces are about the same thickness.

MEASURE UP!

Using the right amount of every ingredient is important, and they are not all measured the same way. To measure liquid ingredients such as broth, water, juice, and milk, use a liquid measuring cup, which is made of glass or plastic and has lines on it to show the amounts, as well as a spout for pouring. Set the measuring cup on the counter and add some liquid. Bend down to make your eyes level with the marks on the cup, and add liquid until it's at the right line.

For dry ingredients such as grated cheese, nuts, flour, sugar, and chopped veggies or fruit, use a dry measuring cup. These are usually made of metal or plastic and come in sets. Each cup is marked with the amount of ingredient it holds when filled to the top. Fill the cup over the top, then use a table knife to level it. Measuring spoons can be used to measure liquid or dry ingredients, and they work the same way—just be sure the ingredient comes to the top of the spoon. Also, never measure ingredients over the bowl or pan in case some extra falls in!

Fuel Your Day

Eating good food keeps you healthy and gives you the energy to concentrate in school, play sports and music, take care of your pets, make art—and have fun with your friends! Barbie makes sure she gets a balance of all of the nutrients she needs every day starting with a good breakfast, eating a healthy lunch, cooking dinner with her family (and sometimes her friends!)—and fueling up with healthy snacks when needed.

There are two main kinds of nutrients you want to be sure to get enough of daily. One kind are called macronutrients. They're the ones you need in larger amounts and include carbohydrates, fat, and protein. Whole grains like brown rice, quinoa, barley, oats, and whole wheat bread and pasta are good sources of carbs. Fat is a good thing when it comes from healthy sources such as olive oil, avocados (eat guacamole!), eggs, and fish such as salmon. Salmon is also a good source of protein, as are beans and legumes (eat hummus!), chicken, lean fish and meat, tofu, and nuts.

The other kind are called micronutrients. You need them in smaller amounts, but they're just as important. Micronutrients include the vitamins and minerals that keep your immune system strong and your bones, skin, hair, and teeth strong and growing. Dairy products such as yogurt, milk, and cheese as well as fruits and vegetables are good sources of micronutrients. When choosing which fruits and veggies to eat, look for the ones that have the darkest or brightest colors—they have the most vitamins and minerals! Good choices include dark leafy greens such as kale, colorful sweet peppers, carrots, broccoli, beets, sweet potatoes, and berries such as blueberries, raspberries, blackberries, and strawberries—as well as fruits such as kiwi and mango.

The best news is that all of these foods aren't only good for you, they're delicious too!

Breakfast Bites

ASK FOR HELP!

Cinnamon-Spiced Buttermilk Waffles

Whether your waffle maker is round, square, or heart-shape, these lightly spiced waffles taste terrific, especially when they're topped with whatever you like best—maple syrup, fresh strawberries, blueberries, raspberries, blackberries, whipped cream, or anything else you can imagine. Cinnamon goes well with chocolate, raspberry, and orange flavors, so a sprinkling of mini chocolate chips or a spoonful of raspberry jam or marmalade might be fun to try too.

MAKE THE BATTER. Heat a waffle iron. Place a heatproof platter in the oven, and preheat the oven to 200°F. In a large bowl, using a sturdy whisk, beat the eggs until evenly mixed. Add the buttermilk, oil, sugar, cinnamon, and baking soda, and whisk together until well combined. Add the flour, baking powder, and salt, and whisk just until the large lumps disappear. Transfer the batter to a large glass measuring pitcher.

COOK THE WAFFLES. When the waffle iron is hot, pour some batter evenly over the center of the grid, spreading it toward, but not into, the corners and edges with a wooden spoon or heatproof spatula. Close the iron and cook according to the manufacturer's directions until the outside of the waffle is golden brown and almost crusty and the inside is soft, light, and springy, about 4 minutes. (The first waffle may not be perfect. Adjust the amount of batter and cooking time for the remaining waffles, if necessary.) Transfer the waffle to the platter in the warm oven to keep warm while you cook the remaining waffles.

TOP THE WAFFLES. Divide the waffles among individual plates and serve with butter, maple syrup, berries, or any of your favorite toppings.

Makes 4–5 servings

2 large eggs

1¾ cups buttermilk

¼ cup canola oil

1 tablespoon sugar

½ teaspoon ground cinnamon

¼ teaspoon baking soda

1½ cups all-purpose flour

2 teaspoons baking powder

⅛ teaspoon salt

Butter, maple syrup, berries, or other favorite topping, for serving

Loaded Avocado Toast

When Barbie goes out to brunch with friends, one of the most popular dishes to order is avocado toast—a crunchy slice of bread topped with creamy avocado and crispy vegetables, and sometimes an egg that's fried, poached, or hard- or soft-boiled. Avocado toast is so easy to make at home, Barbie likes to have the ingredients on hand so she can enoy it anytime—and you can too!

PREPARE THE TOAST. Rub the garlic clove over one side of the toasted bread slice. Arrange the avocado slices in an even layer on the bread, then use a fork to smash the avocado evenly over the entire surface. Season with flaky salt.

TOP THE TOAST. Arrange the egg slices, radish slices, and tomatoes on top in an appealing pattern. Sprinkle with pepper and more salt.

Makes 1 serving

1 clove garlic, lightly smashed

1 thick slice coarse country bread, toasted

½ ripe avocado, halved, pitted, peeled, and sliced

Flaky salt and pepper

1 hard-cooked egg, peeled and thinly sliced (see Tip)

1 radish, thinly sliced

¼ cup multicolor cherry tomatoes, halved

COOKING TIP!
To hard-cook eggs, place eggs in a saucepan with enough water to cover by 1 inch. Bring to a boil over medium-high heat. Remove the pan from the heat, cover, and let stand until done to your liking, about 10 minutes for slightly runny yolks and up to 14 minutes for firm yolks. Drain the eggs, then transfer to a bowl of ice water to cool slightly, 2 minutes or so.

Cheesy Scrambled Eggs in a Mug

ASK FOR HELP!

Need food fast? This is the quickest way to whip up a hearty, high-protein breakfast that will keep you going until lunch. From start to finish, these creamy, cheesy eggs take less than 5 minutes to make. Just add some fresh fruit or fruit juice, and a piece of whole grain toast, if you like, and you are ready to go. You can use any kind of cheese you like or have on hand.

PREPARE THE EGGS. Coat a microwave-safe mug or bowl with cooking spray. Add the eggs and milk to the mug, and whisk until blended. Stir in the cheese, bacon, and onion, and season to taste with salt and pepper.

MICROWAVE THE EGGS. Microwave on high for 45 seconds, stir gently, then continue to microwave until the eggs are nearly set, 30–45 seconds longer. (They will continue to firm up after they are out of the microwave.)

Makes 1 serving

Cooking spray

2 large eggs

2 tablespoons milk

2 tablespoons shredded cheese, such as cheddar or Monterey Jack

2 tablespoons diced cooked bacon

1 teaspoon thinly sliced green onion

Salt and pepper

Berry & Yogurt Parfait

This fruit, yogurt, and granola parfait is as pretty as it is delicious—and it's flexible too. You can really use any type of yogurt, fruit, and granola you like. It never gets boring because you can switch up the ingredients every time you make it.

LAYER THE PARFAIT. Spoon the yogurt into the bottom of a small bowl or parfait glass. Spoon the berries in an even layer on the yogurt. Spoon the granola over the top of the yogurt.

SERVE THE PARFAIT. Serve cold with a spoon for digging down through the layers.

Makes 1 serving

1 container (6 oz) vanilla yogurt

⅓ cup mixed fresh berries, such as blueberries, blackberries, and raspberries

2 tablespoons granola

COOKING TIP!
Swap out the berries for your favorite fruit! Try peeled and sliced kiwi, diced peaches, nectarines, plums, or mandarin orange segments.

Açaí Bowls

So what exactly is açaí, and how do you pronounce it, anyway? Açaí berries come from a type of palm tree that grows in the rainforests of South America, and the word is pronounced "ah-sigh-EE." The berries have a nickname, "purple gold," because they are so good for you. They have lots of vitamins that can help prevent you from getting sick, and they can also help keep your heart and bones strong and healthy.

MAKE THE AÇAÍ PUREE. In a blender, combine the açaí puree, banana, berries, and juice, and blend until very smooth. Divide the mixture evenly between 2 bowls.

TOP THE AÇAÍ BOWL. Top the açaí mixture with your favorite toppings, such as fresh berries, mango slices, banana pieces, kiwi slices, coconut, and chopped nuts or seeds, if you like, and serve right away.

Makes 2 servings

1 packet frozen açaí puree

1 large banana, peeled, roughly chopped, and frozen

1 cup frozen strawberries, blueberries, blackberries, raspberries, or a combination

¼ cup mango juice or other juice of your choice

IDEAS FOR TOPPINGS

¼ cup fresh blueberries, blackberries, raspberries, or strawberries, whole or halved, per bowl

½ cup peeled and thinly sliced mango per bowl

½ cup peeled and thinly sliced banana per bowl

1 kiwi, peeled and thinly sliced, per bowl

2–3 tablespoons lightly toasted shredded or flaked coconut per bowl

2–3 tablespoons chopped pecans or sliced almonds, toasted (optional) per bowl

ASK FOR HELP!

Chia-Seed Pudding with Blackberries, Kiwi & Pomegranate

Pudding for breakfast is totally a go when it's made with tiny-but-mighty chia seeds, which pack in all kinds of good things, like protein for strong muscles and heart-healthy fats. An interesting thing happens when you stir chia seeds into fruit juice or coconut milk: It gets thick and creamy and spoonable—in other words, it turns into pudding!

MAKE THE CHIA PUDDING. In each of 4 half-pint jars, stir together ¼ cup coconut milk, 1 tablespoon chia seeds, 1½ teaspoons maple syrup, and a dash of vanilla. Cover and refrigerate until set, at least 4 hours or overnight.

TOP THE PUDDING. Spoon ½ cup blackberries, ¼ of the kiwi, and ¼ cup pomegranate seeds on top of the pudding in each jar. Sprinkle each with 1 tablespoon coconut chips.

Makes 4 servings

1 cup canned coconut milk

¼ cup chia seeds

2 tablespoons maple syrup

Vanilla extract

2 cups blackberries

1 kiwi, peeled and thinly sliced

1 cup pomegranate seeds

¼ cup toasted coconut chips

COOKING TIPS!

· These puddings are made in pint-size jars and chilled in the refrigerator, so you can make them the night before you want to eat them and they're ready to go the next morning.

· You can find fresh pomegranate seeds with the other fruits and vegetables at the grocery store—or with the frozen fruits too.

· To toast the coconut chips, spread them in a small skillet over medium-low heat and cook for 3 to 6 minutes, stirring every minute or so. They burn quickly, so watch them closely!

Fruit & Nut Overnight Oatmeal

ASK FOR HELP!

A bowl of hot oatmeal is a tasty way to warm up on a cold morning, but this overnight oatmeal can be eaten chilled—right out of the refrigerator—if you like. (Or warm it up for just 1 minute in the microwave.) When you're shopping for oats to make this recipe, look for "old-fashioned oats" on the label. All that means is that the oats are thicker and bigger than "quick oats." Oatmeal made with old-fashioned oats is nice and chewy.

MAKE THE OATMEAL. In each of 2 pint-size jars, stir together ½ cup oats, 1 cup milk, and ½ teaspoon cinnamon. Top each with 2 tablespoons fruit and 2 tablespoons nuts. Screw the lid on each jar, and chill in the refrigerator for at least 4 hours or up to 3 days.

SERVE THE OATMEAL. Enjoy chilled; or remove the lid, cover loosely with a paper towel, and microwave on high for 1 minute to warm. Drizzle honey over the top and stir well. Top with a spoonful of yogurt or applesauce, if using.

Makes 2 servings

1 cup old-fashioned rolled oats

2 cups dairy milk, nut milk, coconut milk, or soy milk

1 teaspoon ground cinnamon

4 tablespoons chopped dried peaches or apricots, or whole fresh blackberries or blueberries, or a combination

4 tablespoons chopped toasted pecans, walnuts, or hazelnuts

2–4 teaspoons honey or other sweetener

Plain yogurt or applesauce (optional)

Awesome Granola

Granola makes a great breakfast, served with any kind of milk you like—dairy, nut, soy, or oat—or layered with yogurt and fruit to make a parfait (see Berry & Yogurt Parfait, page 21). But it makes a wonderful snack too! Barbie likes to keep a small container of homemade granola in her bag or backpack for a quick energy boost when she's at work or school.

PREPARE & PREHEAT. Preheat the oven to 350°F. Line a rimmed baking sheet with parchment paper.

MAKE THE GRANOLA. In a large bowl, combine the oats, pecans, coconut, pepitas, sugar, cinnamon, and salt, and stir to mix well. In a small bowl or cup, whisk together the oil and vanilla. In another small bowl, beat the egg white with a fork until frothy. Pour the oil mixture over the oat mixture and stir to coat evenly. Then pour the egg white over the oat mixture and stir gently until evenly mixed.

BAKE THE GRANOLA. Pour the mixture onto the parchment-lined baking sheet, spreading it evenly over the sheet. Bake the granola, carefully removing the pan from the oven to stir once or twice during baking, until the mixture is nicely toasted, about 35 minutes.

ADD THE FRUIT. Remove from the oven and let cool. Stir in the dried fruit just before serving or storing. Store in an airtight container at room temperature for up to 1 month.

Makes 10–12 servings

2½ cups old-fashioned oats

1 cup chopped pecans

½ cup unsweetened flaked coconut

½ cup raw pepitas (pumpkin seeds)

⅓ cup firmly packed light brown sugar

¾ teaspoon ground cinnamon

¾ teaspoon salt

½ cup canola oil

1 teaspoon vanilla extract

1 large egg white

⅔ cup dried cranberries or golden raisins, or ⅓ cup each

COOKING TIP!
Swap in your own favorite nuts, seeds, and dried fruits—walnuts or almonds, sunflower or sesame seeds, dried blueberries or cherries—in place of what's called for here.

Egg & Cheese Breakfast Tacos

When Barbie hosts friends for a sleepover, she likes to create a top-your-own taco bar for breakfast the next morning. You can do the same thing for your friends! Set out a bowl of scrambled eggs, a couple different kinds of cheese, pico de gallo and/or salsa, and maybe even a few additional toppings such as sliced black olives, chopped green onion, and sour cream—then let everyone dig in! Pico de gallo (pronounced "peek-oh-day-Gy-yo") is a combination of fresh diced tomato, onion, jalapeño, cilantro, lime juice, and salt. You can sometimes find it already made at the grocery store, but it's easy to make your own.

PREPARE THE EGGS. Preheat the oven to 300°F. To make the tacos, stack the tortillas and wrap them in aluminum foil. In a medium bowl, whisk the eggs, ¾ teaspoon salt, and ¼ teaspoon pepper until just nice and frothy, 1–2 minutes.

MAKE THE TACO FILLING. In a large nonstick frying pan, heat the olive oil over medium-high heat. When the oil shimmers, add the onion and cook, stirring often, until the onion has softened, about 2 minutes. Sprinkle with salt and pepper to taste, and reduce the heat to medium-low. Pour in the eggs and cook, without stirring, until they just begin to set, about 20 seconds. Using a silicone spatula, scrape along the bottom and sides of the pan, and fold the egg mixture toward the center of the pan. Continue to cook, scraping and folding the mixture, until the eggs form very moist curds, about 3 minutes longer. Transfer to a large plate, and cover with aluminum foil to keep warm. Meanwhile, place the foil-wrapped tortillas in the oven to warm for 5 minutes.

ASSEMBLE THE TACOS. Remove the tortillas from the oven and unwrap. Place the tortillas on plates. Divide the egg mixture evenly among the tortillas. Sprinkle with cheese and top with pico de gallo and cilantro (if using).

Makes about 4 servings

8 corn or flour tortillas (6 inch)

8 large eggs

Salt and pepper

2 tablespoons olive oil

1 small yellow onion, chopped

1 cup shredded Monterey Jack or cheddar cheese

Pico de gallo or salsa (optional)

Fresh cilantro (optional)

ASK FOR HELP!

Mini Frittatas with Spinach, Bacon & Cheese

These bite-size frittatas are as much fun to make as they are to eat! You will only need about one-quarter of the package of frozen chopped spinach for this recipe, but there are lots of good ways to use the rest of it. Blend it into your breakfast smoothie, stir it into pasta sauce, or add it to a pot of soup.

PREPARE & PREHEAT. Preheat the oven to 375°F. Line a 24-cup mini-muffin pan with foil, paper, or silicone liners, or generously grease the cups with butter. Separate out about one-fourth of the spinach; reserve the rest of the spinach for another use. Using your hands, squeeze the spinach over the sink to get out as much water as you can.

COOK THE FILLING. Set a small frying pan over medium heat. Add the bacon and cook, stirring often, until lightly browned, 3–4 minutes. Using a slotted spoon, transfer the bacon to a paper towel–lined plate; drain off half of the bacon fat and leave the rest in the pan. Set the pan over low heat and add the green onion. Cook, stirring occasionally, until the onion has softened, about 2 minutes. Using the slotted spoon, transfer the onion to the plate with the bacon and set aside.

Makes about 8 servings

Butter, for greasing (optional)

1 package (10 oz) frozen chopped spinach, thawed

4 slices bacon, thinly sliced

2 tablespoons chopped green onion

8 large eggs

2 tablespoons heavy cream

¾ cup shredded Monterey Jack cheese

Salt and pepper

BAKE THE FRITTATAS. In a large bowl, whisk the eggs and cream until blended. Add the cheese, squeezed spinach, and bacon-green onion mixture. Season with a pinch each of salt and pepper, and stir to combine. Divide the egg mixture evenly among the muffin cups. Bake until the frittatas are puffy and set (when the eggs are no longer wobbly), about 10 minutes. Remove from the oven, and let the frittatas cool in the pan on a wire rack for about 5 minutes, then carefully transfer them directly to the rack. Let cool for a few minutes longer, and serve warm or at room temperature.

Buttermilk Banana Pancakes

ASK FOR HELP!

Mashed banana makes these pancakes extra-tender and gives them yummy banana flavor. Be sure you use a banana that is nice and ripe—it should have black speckles all over it and feel slightly soft when you press on it with your fingers.

MIX THE INGREDIENTS. In a medium bowl, whisk the egg until foamy. Add the buttermilk, mashed banana, and 2 tablespoons melted butter, and whisk gently just to combine. Add the flour, sugar, baking powder, baking soda, and salt, and whisk gently just until the flour is mixed in. (To make plain buttermilk pancakes, omit the banana and increase the amount of buttermilk to 2½ cups.)

COOK THE PANCAKES. Heat a large frying pan or griddle over medium heat until hot but not smoking. Add a little bit of butter to the pan and, using a spatula, spread it evenly over the bottom. For each pancake, spoon ¼-cup portions of the batter onto the pan a few inches apart. Cook until the edges of the pancakes begin to look dry and the bottoms are golden brown, about 2 minutes. Slide a spatula underneath each pancake and carefully flip it over to cook the other side. Cook the pancakes on their second side until golden brown on the bottom and the batter is no longer runny in the center, about 1 minute longer. Cook the remaining pancakes the same way.

SERVE THE PANCAKES. Using the spatula, slide the pancakes onto a serving plate. Serve warm with butter and syrup to drizzle over the top.

Makes 4–6 servings

1 large egg

2 cups buttermilk

1 ripe banana, mashed

2 tablespoons butter, melted, plus more for cooking the pancakes and serving

1 cup all-purpose flour

1 tablespoon sugar

1 teaspoon baking powder

½ teaspoon baking soda

½ teaspoon salt

Maple syrup, for serving

Peanut Butter & Jelly Muffins

If you're like Barbie, you have more than one best friend, but lots of people would say peanut butter has just one BFF: jelly. You can use any jelly or jam you like in these muffins, or substitute almond or cashew butter for the peanut butter.

PREPARE & PREHEAT. Preheat the oven to 375°F. Grease a standard 12-cup muffin pan with softened butter.

MIX THE DRY INGREDIENTS. In a large bowl, stir together the flour, sugar, baking powder, baking soda, and salt.

MIX THE WET INGREDIENTS. In another large bowl, whisk together the 6 tablespoons melted butter, the eggs, vanilla, and sour cream until smooth. Add the egg mixture to the dry ingredients and stir just until evenly moistened. The batter will be slightly lumpy. Do not overmix.

FILL THE MUFFIN CUPS. Spoon the batter into each muffin cup, filling it one-third full. Drop a heaping ½ teaspoonful each of peanut butter and jelly into the center of each cup, then cover with batter.

BAKE THE MUFFINS. Bake until golden and springy to the touch, 20–25 minutes. Transfer the pan to a wire rack and let cool for 5 minutes. Carefully remove the muffins from the pan. Serve warm or at room temperature.

Makes 12 servings

6 tablespoons unsalted butter, melted, plus more softened butter for greasing

2 cups all-purpose flour

¾ cup sugar

1 tablespoon baking powder

½ teaspoon baking soda

½ teaspoon salt

2 large eggs

1¼ teaspoons vanilla extract

1¼ cups sour cream

Peanut butter

Jelly or seedless jam of your choice

Bite-Size Berry Scones

These tiny treats are perfect with fresh fruit or eggs for breakfast, or with tea, hot chocolate, or a glass of milk for an afternoon snack.

PREPARE & PREHEAT. Preheat the oven to 425°F. Line a baking sheet with parchment paper.

MAKE THE DOUGH. In a large bowl, whisk together the 3 cups flour, the granulated sugar, baking powder, baking soda, and salt. Scatter the butter pieces over the flour mixture and toss to coat. Using a pastry blender or 2 table knives, cut the butter into the dry ingredients until the mixture forms crumbs about the size of small peas. Stir in the dried berries. Pour in the buttermilk and stir with a fork or rubber spatula just until combined. (For scones that are perfectly tender and not tough, be sure the butter and buttermilk are cold, knead the dough gently, and work quickly so the dough doesn't get too soft.)

SHAPE THE DOUGH. Sprinkle a clean work surface with flour, and turn the dough out onto the floured surface. With floured hands, gently knead the dough 8–10 times; the dough will be very soft. Press and pat the dough into a rectangle about ¾ inch thick. Using a 1½-inch biscuit cutter or shaped cookie cutter, cut out as many rounds of dough as possible. Gather up the scraps, knead just a little bit, and pat to ¾ inch thick. Cut out more rounds and place them on the prepared baking sheet, spacing them evenly.

BAKE THE SCONES. Bake until the edges are golden brown, about 10 minutes. Remove from the oven, and carefully transfer them to a wire rack to cool.

MAKE THE GLAZE. In a small bowl, whisk together the powdered sugar and milk until smooth; it should be thick but pourable. If needed, whisk in additional milk 1 teaspoon at a time. Brush or drizzle over the warm scones. Let stand for at least 10 minutes to allow the glaze to set. Serve warm or at room temperature.

Makes about 12 servings

FOR THE SCONES

3 cups all-purpose flour, plus more for dusting

3 tablespoons granulated sugar

2½ teaspoons baking powder

½ teaspoon baking soda

½ teaspoon salt

10 tablespoons (1¼ sticks) cold unsalted butter, cut into ½-inch pieces

¾ cup dried cranberries or dried blueberries

1 cup cold buttermilk

FOR THE GLAZE

¾ cup powdered sugar, sifted

1 tablespoon whole milk or water, plus more as needed

Savory Snacks

Veggies with Green Goddess Dip

This snack is a rainbow on a plate! It's the perfect thing to serve at your next pizza party for something fresh and crunchy. Watercress is a kind of leafy green. It has a little bit of a peppery flavor—but not too much! If you can't find it, you can use baby arugula instead. It's another kind of green that is just a little bit peppery. When it's mixed with the yogurt and other ingredients, it just makes the dip taste good!

MAKE THE DIP. In a food processor or blender, combine the yogurt, watercress, dill, green onion, sugar, salt, and hot pepper sauce (if using). Cover and process until smooth. Pour the dip into a container, cover, and refrigerate for a few hours. The dip will be thin when you first make it, but it will thicken in the refrigerator. Shake or stir well before serving. The dip will keep for up to 3 days.

BOIL THE POTATOES. Fill a large saucepan about three-fourths full of water, and add the salt and potatoes. Set the pan over medium-high heat and bring to a boil. Reduce the heat to medium-low and simmer, uncovered, until the potatoes are tender when you poke them with a fork, about 20 minutes. Drain the potatoes in a colander set in the sink. Let cool completely.

SERVE THE VEGGIES & DIP. On a large platter, arrange the potatoes, carrots, green beans, radishes, and cucumber sticks. Put the dip in a bowl and serve with the veggies. (You could also fill the platter with other favorite veggies— sugar snap peas and cherry tomatoes would be tasty with the dip too.)

Makes 4–6 servings

FOR THE DIP

1 cup plain whole milk Greek yogurt

1 cup watercress leaves and tender stems or baby arugula

2 tablespoons chopped fresh dill

1 green onion, thinly sliced

½ teaspoon sugar

½ teaspoon salt

⅛ teaspoon hot pepper sauce (optional)

FOR THE VEGGIES

1 tablespoon salt

6 small new or rainbow potatoes, halved or quartered lengthwise

12 small rainbow carrots, halved lengthwise

½ lb green beans, stem ends trimmed

12 small assorted radishes, whole, halved, quartered, or sliced

2 mini cucumbers, quartered lengthwise and cut into 3-inch sticks

Sweet Potato Oven Fries

ASK FOR HELP!

These fries are a perfect side dish to a burger or delicious on their own, and they have a lot of good nutrition in them too. It's nice to season them with a salt that has a bit of texture. There's a kind called kosher salt available at any grocery store that will do nicely!

PREPARE THE POTATOES. Preheat the oven to 450°F. Rinse and dry the sweet potatoes, but do not peel them. Cut the sweet potatoes lengthwise into slices ½ inch thick, then cut each slice into long sticks about ¼ inch wide. Arrange the sticks in a single layer on a rimmed baking sheet, and toss with the olive oil and ⅛ teaspoon salt. Roast, stirring halfway through baking time, until tender and browned on the edges, 20–25 minutes.

SEASON & SERVE THE FRIES. Remove the fries from the oven. Transfer the potatoes to a heatproof bowl. Stir together the parsley and garlic, and mix gently to coat the fries. Season to taste with more salt, if needed. Serve with ketchup.

Makes about 3 servings

1 lb sweet potatoes

1 tablespoon olive oil

⅛ teaspoon coarse salt, plus more for seasoning (optional)

1 tablespoon chopped fresh flat-leaf parsley

1 clove garlic, minced

Ketchup

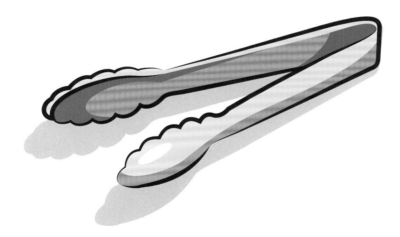

ASK FOR HELP!

Turkey, Cheese & Salsa Pinwheels

With protein and carbohydrates and yummy melted cheese, these spiraled treats will give you energy before you head off to soccer practice or dance class!

PREHEAT THE OVEN TO 350°F. Place the tortilla on a baking sheet and sprinkle the cheese over the top. Bake until the cheese melts, about 5 minutes. Arrange the turkey slices over the cheese, and then top with a few spoonfuls of salsa and/or mashed avocado (f using). Roll up the tortilla into a tight cylinder. Trim the ends, and then cut the cylinder crosswise into slices.

Makes 4 servings

1 flour tortilla (10 inch)

2 oz Monterey Jack cheese

4 slices deli turkey

Salsa (optional)

1 avocado, mashed (optional)

Smoked Salmon & Cucumber Pinwheels

These pinwheels are just a little bit fancy—perfect for a tea party snack!

MIX TOGETHER THE CREAM CHEESE & CHIVES. Spread the cream cheese evenly over the tortilla. Cover with a layer of salmon. Draw a vegetable peeler along the cucumber to create 6 thin slices. Arrange the cucumber slices over the salmon. Roll up the tortilla into a tight cylinder. Trim the ends, and then cut the cylinder crosswise into slices.

Makes 4 servings

2 tablespoons cream cheese, softened

1 teaspoon minced fresh chives

1 flour tortilla (10 inch)

4 oz smoked salmon, thinly sliced

½ English cucumber, peeled

COOKING TIP!
For this recipe, you want what's called an English cucumber. You'll find them with the other cucumbers in the grocery store. They're long and thin and usually come wrapped in plastic. They are crunchier than regular cucumbers, and their seeds are so tiny, you can't see or taste them.

Broccoli-Apple Slaw

When you're craving some crunch, this colorful slaw tossed in a creamy avocado dressing hits the spot! Barbie likes to serve it as a side dish when she heads out in her DreamCamper with friends and grilled chicken or bratwurst is on the campout menu!

MAKE THE DRESSING. In a bowl, use a fork to mash the avocado until smooth. Add the yogurt, lemon juice, and mustard, and stir until well blended. Season to taste with salt and pepper.

ASSEMBLE THE SLAW. In a large bowl, combine the broccoli slaw, apple, and cranberries, and toss to mix well. Add the dressing, and toss until the broccoli and fruits are evenly coated.

FINISH & SERVE THE SLAW. Transfer the slaw to a serving plate, top with the cashews, and serve.

Makes about 4 servings

FOR THE DRESSING

1 avocado, halved, pitted, and peeled

2 tablespoons plain Greek yogurt

2 tablespoons fresh lemon juice

1 teaspoon Dijon mustard

Salt and pepper

FOR THE SLAW

½ (12 oz) package broccoli slaw

½ large Honeycrisp apple, cored and diced

½ cup dried cranberries

½ cup roasted cashews, chopped

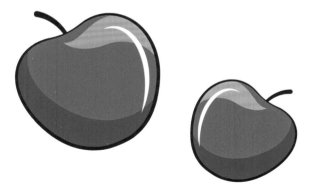

Ceviche with Lime & Herbs

Ceviche (pronounced "seh-VEE-chay") is a refreshing and flavorful dish of marinated fish that's enjoyed in many Spanish-speaking countries. You will see that as the fish soaks in the lime juice mixture in the refrigerator, it turns white. That's because the lime juice cooks it—without any heat! Be sure your fish is very fresh for this recipe.

MARINATE THE FISH. In a bowl, stir together the fish pieces, lime juice, onion, and jalapeño. Cover and refrigerate until the fish is opaque throughout, 30–60 minutes.

MAKE THE CEVICHE. Using a slotted spoon, transfer the fish, onion, and jalapeño to another bowl, leaving the liquid behind. Stir in the avocado, cilantro, and mint, and season with salt and pepper. Taste, and add some of the marinade, if you like, for more flavor. Serve with tortilla chips.

Makes 6 servings

1 lb boneless firm white-flesh fish, such as snapper or halibut, cut into ½-inch pieces

1⅓ cups fresh lime juice

¼ cup minced white onion

1 jalapeño chile, seeded and minced

1 avocado, halved, pitted, peeled, and diced

¼ cup chopped fresh cilantro

2 tablespoons finely chopped fresh mint

Salt and pepper

Tortilla chips, for serving

Zucchini Fritters

 ASK FOR HELP!

When the summer garden at Sweet Orchard Farm is bursting with zucchini, Barbie likes to make these lacy little pancakes flavored with Parmesan cheese, garlic, green onion, and parsley. For the crispiest fritters, squeeze out as much water from the grated zucchini as you can.

PREPARE THE ZUCCHINI. Use a box grater to grate the zucchini into a bowl. Toss the zucchini and salt, and let sit for 10 minutes. Wrap the shredded zucchini in a clean cotton kitchen towel, and squeeze it over the sink to drain the excess liquid.

MAKE THE FRITTERS. In a large bowl, combine the zucchini, egg, cheese, garlic, onion, parsley, and pepper to taste. Sprinkle the flour and baking powder evenly over the mixture, and stir until just incorporated.

COOK THE FRITTERS. Heat the olive oil over medium-high heat. Spoon portions of about 1 tablespoon of the zucchini mixture into the pan. Use the back of a spatula to flatten the mounds, and cook until deep golden brown, about 2–3 minutes. Flip and cook the other side until golden brown, about 2–3 minutes more, then transfer to a plate. Repeat with remaining zucchini mixture. Serve with Greek yogurt (if using).

Makes 4–5 servings

1 zucchini

½ teaspoon salt

1 large egg, beaten

3 tablespoons grated Parmesan cheese

1 clove garlic, minced

1 green onion, finely chopped

¼ teaspoon dried parsley

Pepper

¼ cup all-purpose flour

¼ teaspoon baking powder

2 tablespoons olive oil

Greek yogurt, for dipping (optional)

Hummus with Root Chip Dippers

Digging into this creamy dip with colorful "chips" is a great way to get your veggies in. To make the hummus, you will need an ingredient called tahini. It is made from ground sesame seeds—the same way peanut butter is made from ground peanuts. You can find it at almost any grocery store. If you have leftover hummus, eat it with pita wedges or in a sandwich or wrap.

CUT THE CHIPS. Fill a large bowl with ice water. Very carefully, slice the radishes, carrots, and beet, working with one type of vegetable at a time. As the "chips" are cut, transfer them to the ice water. Let the vegetables stand in the water for at least 20 minutes, or cover and refrigerate for up to 1 day.

Makes about 8 servings

FOR THE ROOT
VEGETABLE CHIPS

3 large radishes

2 large rainbow carrots, peeled

1 small golden beet, peeled

MAKE THE HUMMUS. In a food processor or blender, combine the chickpeas, lemon juice, tahini, oil, garlic, cumin, and salt. Process until a soft, creamy paste forms. Taste and adjust the seasoning with more salt and lemon juice if you'd like.

SERVE WITH CHIPS. Transfer the hummus to a serving bowl. Drain the root chips, pat dry with a paper towel, and arrange on a serving platter with the hummus.

FOR THE HUMMUS

2 cans (15 oz each) chickpeas, drained and rinsed

½ cup fresh lemon juice, plus more if needed

½ cup tahini (sesame paste)

3 tablespoons olive oil

5 cloves garlic, minced

¼ teaspoon ground cumin

¾ teaspoon salt

Dressed-Up Popcorn

ASK FOR HELP!

Settle in at your next movie party with a big bowl of tasty popcorn you can fancy up with your choice of ranch seasoning, Parmesan cheese, or dried cranberries, peanuts, chocolate chips, and maple syrup to make an awesome sweet-and-salty trail mix!

POP THE CORN. In a large, heavy-bottom pan with a tight-fitting lid, warm the oil over medium heat. Add the popcorn and cover the pan. Don't touch the pan until you hear the first few pops, then shake the pan and continue to cook, shaking the pan every 20 seconds or so, until the popping slows way, way down, about 6 minutes. Remove from the heat.

DRESS THE POPCORN. While the popcorn is still hot, toss it with your choice of the following flavor combinations:

RANCH: In a large bowl, stir together 2 tablespoons each melted butter and freshly grated Parmesan cheese; ½ teaspoon each onion powder, dried dill, and salt; and ¼ teaspoon garlic powder. Add the hot popcorn, and toss to mix.

TRAIL MIX: In a large bowl, toss together 2 tablespoons melted butter and the hot popcorn. Add ½ cup each dried cranberries and salted peanuts, ¼ cup chocolate chips (any kind), and 2 tablespoons maple syrup; toss to mix.

CHEESY: In a large bowl, toss together 3 tablespoons melted butter and 1 teaspoon salt. Add the hot popcorn, and toss to coat evenly. Sprinkle 1 cup grated Parmesan cheese over the buttered popcorn, and toss to mix.

Makes 4–6 servings

2 tablespoons canola oil

½ cup unpopped popcorn

Party Snack Mix

You can buy the stuff that comes in a bag, but it's easy—and so much tastier, not to mention healthier—to make your own!

MAKE THE MIX. Preheat the oven to 250°F. Put the butter in a shallow baking dish and set in the oven until melted. Stir in the Worcestershire sauce, sugar, seasoned salt, onion powder, and garlic powder until blended. Add the cereal, nuts, pretzels, and crackers, and toss gently but thoroughly to coat with the seasoned butter.

BAKE THE MIX. Spread the cereal mixture evenly in the dish and bake for 45 minutes, stirring every 10 minutes. Let cool. Pack in an airtight container and store for up to 2 weeks.

Makes about 6 servings

2 tablespoons butter

1 tablespoon Worcestershire sauce

1 teaspoon sugar

1 teaspoon seasoned salt

½ teaspoon onion powder

¼ teaspoon garlic powder

2 cups bite-size square cereal, in any combination of wheat, rice, and/or corn

¼ cup mixed nuts

¼ cup bite-size pretzels

¼ cup bite-size cheddar crackers

Crispy Chickpeas

Versatile chickpeas (also called garbanzo beans) are the main ingredient in hummus (page 47). Here, they are seasoned and roasted to make a crunchy snack.

SEASON THE CHICKPEAS. Preheat the oven to 400°F. Spread the chickpeas on paper towels and pat them dry. Transfer to a bowl, add the oil, and toss to coat evenly. Sprinkle on the cumin, chili powder, and salt, and toss to mix evenly. Spread the chickpeas in an even layer on a rimmed baking sheet.

ROAST THE CHICKPEAS. Roast the chickpeas, shaking the pan every 10 minutes to ensure they brown evenly, until crispy and lightly browned, 30–40 minutes. Let cool completely on the pan on a wire rack. Store any leftovers in an airtight container at room temperature for up to 5 days.

Makes 6–8 servings

2 cans (15 oz each) chickpeas, drained and rinsed

1 tablespoon olive oil

2 teaspoons ground cumin

2 teaspoons chili powder or smoked paprika

1 teaspoon salt

COOKING TIP!
Switch up the seasonings! Add 1 teaspoon garlic powder to the mix, or substitute ground turmeric and ginger for the cumin and chili powder.

Guacamole

Take this always-popular avocado dip to your next party and watch it disappear! To get the best avocados, buy them when they're bright green and slightly hard. Let them sit on your counter for a few days, until they're dark green on the outside and feel slightly soft when you press them with your fingers. Be sure to ask an adult to help you get the pit out—it can be tricky. The safest way is to use a spoon to scoop out the big pit.

MASH THE AVOCADO. In a bowl, combine the avocados, lime juice, and garlic. Using a fork, mash the mixture until just smooth, leaving some chunky avocado bits for texture. Add the tomato and stir to blend. Add a few dashes of the hot pepper sauce and a sprinkling of salt and pepper.

SERVE THE GUACAMOLE. Spoon the guacamole into a serving bowl, and serve at room temperature with the tortilla chips and/or vegetables.

Makes 4–6 servings

2 ripe avocados, halved, pitted, peeled, and diced

2 teaspoons fresh lime juice

2 garlic cloves, minced

½ plum tomato, chopped

Hot pepper sauce

Salt and pepper

Tortilla chips and/or vegetable sticks for dipping

COOKING TIP!
For extra zing, try adding finely chopped onion, minced jalapeño chile, or chopped fresh cilantro to the mix.

Soups & Salads

Summery Minestrone

Minestrone (pronounced "mih-nuh-STROW-nee") is an Italian vegetable soup with pasta and white beans. You can use any kind of white beans here—cannellini, navy beans, or Great Northern beans. After you've topped your soup with pesto, take a big sniff—it smells so good!

COOK THE ONION & TOMATOES. In a frying pan over medium heat, warm the oil. Add the onion and cook, stirring occasionally, until softened, about 5 minutes. Add the tomatoes and their juice, and cook, stirring, until the tomatoes are tender, about 8 minutes. Remove from the heat.

SIMMER THE SOUP. In a large saucepan, combine the broth, tomato mixture, carrots, potatoes, leeks, and celery. Bring to a boil over high heat, reduce the heat to medium-low, and simmer gently for 15 minutes. Add the green beans, zucchini, pasta, and white beans, and simmer until the vegetables and pasta are tender, about 10 minutes.

SERVE. Ladle the soup into individual bowls, and top each serving with a spoonful of pesto.

Makes 8 servings

1 tablespoon canola oil

1 yellow onion, chopped

1 can (14 oz) diced tomatoes with juice

8 cups chicken broth

4 carrots, peeled and thinly sliced

2 Yukon gold potatoes, diced

2 leeks, white parts only, thinly sliced

2 large celery ribs with leaves, thinly sliced

4 oz green beans, trimmed and cut into 1-inch pieces (about 2 cups)

1 zucchini or yellow summer squash, sliced

1 cup small pasta shells, fusilli, or other small shape

1 cup drained canned white beans, rinsed

Store-bought pesto

COOKING TIP!
Feel free to swap out or add whatever vegetables you like to this soup. Sugar snap peas, mushrooms, and cauliflower are just a few of the possibilities.

Miso Soup with Soba Noodles, Tofu & Mushrooms

Miso (pronounced "MEE-so") soup is a light and comforting Japanese dish. It's usually made with a special broth called dashi, made with dried and smoked fish and seaweed. This recipe calls for chicken or mushroom broth to make it a little easier! If you can't find miso paste at your regular grocery store, look for it at an Asian market.

PREPARE THE TOFU. Drain the tofu and slice in half crosswise. Place both pieces of tofu on a paper towel-lined plate. Top with another paper towel and a second plate. Weigh down the top plate with a heavy can. Let stand for 20 minutes to drain the tofu. Cut the tofu into tiny cubes. Set aside.

BOIL THE NOODLES. Meanwhile, bring a pot of salted water to a boil over high heat. Add the soba noodles and cook, stirring occasionally, until tender but still a little firm, about 6 minutes. Add the mushrooms and carrot during the last 30 seconds of cooking. Drain, rinse under cold water, and drain again. Leave the noodles and vegetables in the strainer. Set aside.

HEAT THE BROTH. In a medium saucepan, bring the chicken broth to a boil over medium heat. Add the noodles, sliced vegetables, and tofu, and rewarm over low heat.

ADD THE MISO. Transfer ¼ cup of the warm broth to a small bowl, add the miso paste, and stir until smooth. Add the miso mixture to the saucepan and warm gently; do not boil. Divide the noodles, tofu, and vegetables evenly among 4 small soup bowls, then pour in the broth, dividing it evenly. Sprinkle with the green onion.

Makes 4 servings

2 oz firm tofu

4 oz dried soba noodles

2 oz small white mushrooms, thinly sliced

1 small carrot, peeled and thinly sliced

3 cups chicken broth or mushroom broth

¼ cup white miso paste

1 small green onion, thinly sliced

Broccoli & Cheddar Soup

When you're good and hungry, this hearty, cheesy soup will fill you up. (And it's a yummy way to eat broccoli!) To be safe, be sure to let the hot broth and cooked broccoli mixture cool for 30 minutes before blending it. The blended mixture is reheated when milk is added to help make the soup creamy, so it will still be nice and hot when you serve it.

PREPARE THE BROCCOLI. Use a vegetable peeler to peel away the tough outer layer of the broccoli stems. Coarsely chop the broccoli florets (the flowery top part) and stems.

MAKE THE SOUP. Pour the broth into a medium saucepan. Set the pan over high heat and bring to a boil. Reduce the heat to medium-low to maintain a gentle simmer. Place a large saucepan over medium heat and add the butter. When the butter has melted, add the onion and cook, stirring often, until soft, about 8 minutes. Sprinkle in the flour and cook, stirring often, for 1 minute longer. Carefully add the broth, broccoli, lemon juice, and thyme. Bring to a boil. Reduce the heat to low, cover, and simmer until the broccoli is tender, about 20 minutes. Remove the pan from the heat. Let the broccoli mixture cool until it's lukewarm, about 30 minutes.

BLEND THE SOUP. Transfer one-third to one-half of the broccoli mixture to a blender. Cover and blend until smooth. Repeat with remaining broccoli mixture, pouring each batch into a large bowl until all the soup is blended. Return all of the soup to the saucepan. Stir in the milk, and bring to a gentle simmer over low heat. Sprinkle half of the cheese into the soup and stir until melted. Taste the soup (careful, it's hot!) and season with salt and pepper.

SERVE. Ladle the soup into bowls, and top with the rest of the cheese.

Makes 6–8 servings

1½ lb broccoli

5 cups chicken broth

2 tablespoons butter

1 yellow onion, finely chopped

¼ cup all-purpose flour

1 tablespoon fresh lemon juice

½ teaspoon dried thyme

2 cups whole milk

½ lb sharp cheddar cheese, shredded

Salt and pepper

Easy Tomato Soup

ASK FOR HELP!

This light tomato soup is delicious paired with grilled cheese for dipping (of course!). For each sandwich, butter both sides of two pieces of bread. Top one bread slice with 2 slices of American or cheddar cheese, then cover with the other bread slice. Cook in a nonstick skillet over medium heat until the bread is toasted and the cheese is melty, about 4 minutes on each side.

COOK THE VEGETABLES. In a large saucepan over medium heat, warm the oil and butter. Add the onion and cook, stirring often, until softened, 5–7 minutes. Add the garlic and cook, stirring, for 2 minutes. Add the tomatoes and their juice and the broth. Turn the heat to high, and bring to a boil. Reduce the heat to medium-low and simmer, stirring occasionally, for 20 minutes.

BLEND THE SOUP. Remove the pan from the heat. Let the tomato mixture cool until it's lukewarm, about 30 minutes. Transfer one-third to one-half of the tomato mixture to a blender. Cover and blend until smooth. Repeat with the remaining tomato mixture, pouring each batch into a large bowl until all the soup is blended. Return all of the soup to the saucepan.

REHEAT & SERVE. Return the saucepan to medium-low heat. Stir well, then season with the salt and pepper. Heat, stirring, until steaming. Ladle the soup into individual bowls.

Makes 6 servings

1 tablespoon olive oil

2 tablespoons butter

1 yellow onion, coarsely chopped

2 cloves garlic, minced

1 can (28 oz) diced tomatoes with juice

4 cups chicken broth or vegetable broth

½ teaspoon salt

½ teaspoon pepper

ASK FOR HELP!

Cool Cucumber-Dill Soup

Soup isn't always served hot. This pretty pale-green chilled soup is super refreshing on a hot summer day. It's nice served with light and crispy crackers or toasted pita chips.

MAKE THE SOUP. Coarsely chop 5 of the cucumber halves and transfer to a large bowl. Add the yogurt, lemon juice, green onions, dill, garlic, caraway seeds, salt, and pepper. Stir to combine, cover, and set aside at room temperature for 1 hour to blend the flavors. Dice the remaining cucumber piece. Set aside.

BLEND THE SOUP. Transfer one-third to one-half of the cucumber mixture to a blender. Cover the blender, but remove the small plastic cap in the center of the lid. With the machine running, slowly add a little bit of the broth through the opening and blend until smooth. Pour into a container. Repeat with the remaining cucumber mixture and broth. Stir to blend everything together. Cover and refrigerate until well chilled, about 2 hours.

SERVE. Just before serving, stir in the oil. Pour the soup into individual bowls. Garnish with diced cucumber and additional fresh dill.

Makes 6 servings

3 English cucumbers, halved lengthwise and seeded (see Tip, page 42)

1 cup plain whole milk Greek yogurt

1 tablespoon lemon juice

3 green onions, chopped

3 tablespoons chopped fresh dill, plus more for garnish

1 clove garlic, chopped

1 teaspoon caraway seeds

1 teaspoon salt

¼ teaspoon ground white pepper

1 cup chicken broth or vegetable broth

2 tablespoons olive oil

Rainbow Carrot Ribbon Salad

This pretty salad may look hard to make, but it couldn't be easier. All you need is a vegetable peeler. Rainbow carrots got their name because they can be orange, yellow, dark red, white, or purple. No matter their color, all carrots taste the same—sweet and crunchy!

MAKE THE CARROT RIBBONS. Place a carrot flat on a work surface. Holding the top end of the carrot with one hand, use a vegetable peeler to peel thin strips off the carrot lengthwise. As you work, rotate the carrot to peel it evenly. Stop making the ribbons when the center of the carrot is too thin to hold steady. Transfer the ribbons to a large bowl or plate. Repeat with the the remaining carrots.

ASSEMBLE THE SALAD. Put the lettuce on the bottom of a large bowl. Arrange the cucumber slices on top, followed by the carrot ribbons. Set aside.

Makes 6 servings

1 lb rainbow carrots (about 8), peeled

1 head red or green leaf lettuce or romaine lettuce, cored and chopped

1 English cucumber, sliced (see Tip, page 42)

½ cup pepitas (pumpkin seeds), toasted

MAKE THE DRESSING. In a bowl, whisk together the yogurt, mayonnaise, buttermilk, lemon juice, dill, parsley, and salt.

DRESS & SERVE THE SALAD. If you will be serving all of the salad at once, pour about 1 cup of the dressing over the salad; then, using 2 large spoons, toss it with the vegetables to coat them evenly. Sprinkle the pumpkin seeds on top, and serve the remaining dressing alongside. Or you can serve portions of the salad in small bowls. Pour a few tablespoons of the dressing on top of each portion, and then sprinkle some pumpkin seeds on top. Leftover undressed salad and dressing can be packed into separate airtight containers and stored in the refrigerator for up to 3 days.

FOR THE DRESSING

½ cup plain whole milk Greek yogurt

½ cup mayonnaise

⅓ cup buttermilk

2 tablespoons lemon juice

1 tablespoon chopped fresh dill

1 tablespoon chopped fresh flat-leaf parsley

½ teaspoon salt

Taco Salad

ASK FOR HELP!

When you're hungry and you need something tasty and satisfying—fast!—this salad is just the thing. Simply toss together the lettuce, tomato, beans (you pick), and black olives, and drizzle with a salsa-sour cream dressing. A topping of shredded cheese and crumbled tortilla chips adds extra crunch.

MAKE THE DRESSING. In a small bowl, stir together the salsa and sour cream. In another small bowl, combine the cheese and crumbled tortilla chips.

MAKE THE SALAD. In a large bowl, combine the lettuce, tomato, beans, and olives. Toss to combine. Serve topped with the dressing and chip-cheese mixture.

Makes 1–2 servings

2 tablespoons salsa

1 tablespoon sour cream

¼ cup shredded Monterey Jack cheese

⅓ cup crumbled tortilla chips

1½ cups shredded lettuce

¼ cup chopped tomato

¼ cup canned black, kidney, or pinto beans, drained and rinsed

2 tablespoons sliced black olives

Watermelon, Mango & Avocado Salad with Mint & Lime

This super-fresh salad calls for a lot of cutting with a sharp knife. Be sure to have an adult help you with that—then you can arrange everything on a platter however you think it looks best. Let your creativity loose!

DICE THE WATERMELON. Cut the watermelon in quarters. Using a large, sharp knife, cut away the rind by following the shape of the fruit. Repeat with the three other quarters. Throw away the rinds. Cut the watermelon quarters into 1-inch slices, then lay the slices flat and cut into ½-inch cubes. Arrange on a serving platter.

DICE THE MANGO. Hold the mango upright on a cutting board. Using the same large knife, cut down through the mango, top to bottom, just to one side of the center to cut the mango flesh from the pit. Repeat on the other side. Using a small, sharp knife, cut off the mango peel, dice the fruit, and add to the platter.

DICE THE AVOCADO. Using the small knife, cut into the center of the avocado, cutting all the way around the avocado when you reach the big round pit in the center. Separate the avocado halves. Use the tip of a spoon to remove the pit, then remove the peel and dice the avocado. Add the avocado to the platter.

ADD THE LIME. Sprinkle the lime zest and juice all over the fruit. Toss gently with your hands to mix. Garnish the salad with the nuts and mint.

Makes 6 servings

1 small seedless watermelon, about 3 lb (about 3 cups cubed watermelon)

1 ripe mango

1 avocado

Grated zest and juice of 1 lime

¼ cup chopped pistachios or toasted sliced almonds

6 fresh mint leaves, torn into small pieces

Crunchy Quinoa Salad with Lemon Vinaigrette

When Barbie packs a picnic lunch for a day at the beach, this lemony grain-and-veggie salad is one of her favorites. Not only is it delicious, but it keeps well on the way there. If you'd like to take it on your next adventure, pack it in a tightly sealed container in a cooler to keep it fresh—and give it a good stir before you serve it!

MAKE THE QUINOA. In a small saucepan, combine the quinoa, water, and salt, and bring to a boil over high heat. Reduce the heat to low. Stir, cover, and cook, without lifting the lid, until the liquid is absorbed and the quinoa is tender, about 15 minutes. Remove from the heat and let stand, covered, for 5 minutes. Uncover and fluff with a fork, then cover and let cool to room temperature.

MAKE THE SALAD. While the quinoa cools, make the vinaigrette. In a jar with a lid, combine the lemon juice, vinegar, and oil. Cover and shake until evenly blended. Season to taste with salt and pepper. In a large bowl, combine the quinoa, kale, carrots, pomegranate seeds, mint, almonds, sesame seeds, and vinaigrette. Toss to mix evenly.

Makes 4 servings

FOR THE SALAD

1 cup quinoa, rinsed

2 cups water or chicken broth

½ teaspoon salt

2 cups baby kale

2 small carrots, thinly sliced

¼ cup pomegranate seeds

2 tablespoons fresh mint leaves

2 tablespoons toasted sliced almonds or roasted sunflower seeds

1 tablespoon sesame seeds

FOR THE VINAIGRETTE

2 tablespoons fresh lemon juice

1 tablespoon white wine vinegar

¼ cup olive oil

Salt and pepper

Caprese Salad

One of Barbie's favorite summer activities is going to the farmers' market, where she can find the freshest, most beautiful fruits and vegetables—like the tomatoes to make this Italian salad—and maybe even talk to the farmer who grew them. If you don't grow your own tomatoes, ask an adult if there's a farmer's market close to where you live. You can make this salad with tomatoes from the grocery store too—just try to find the ripest ones you can.

CUT THE TOMATOES. Place the tomatoes on a cutting board, stem sides down. Using a sharp knife, make 4 evenly spaced slits crosswise in each tomato, stopping about ½ inch from the bottom.

CUT THE CHEESE. Cut the cheese into 16 thin, evenly sized slices. Working with 1 tomato at a time, insert 1 cheese slice and 1 basil leaf into each slit.

SERVE THE SALAD. When you're ready to serve, place the stuffed tomatoes on a platter. Drizzle with olive oil and season with salt and pepper.

Makes 4 servings

4 large ripe tomatoes

2 balls fresh mozzarella cheese (about 5 oz total weight)

16 fresh basil leaves

Olive oil, for drizzling

Salt and pepper

COOKING TIP!
You can slice and arrange this salad any way you like—stuff whole tomatoes with mozzarella and basil leaves; layer big rounds; or toss grape tomatoes with tiny balls of fresh mozzarella called bocconcini.

Fresh Strawberry & Spinach Salad

ASK FOR HELP!

If you ever need to get someone who says they don't like salad to try salad, make this! Not only is it pretty, but the combination of tender baby spinach, sweet strawberries, and crunchy toasted pecans all tossed in a lightly sweet poppy seed dressing is a real winner.

TOAST THE PECANS. In a dry frying pan, toast the pecans over medium-low heat, stirring, until fragrant and starting to brown, about 5 minutes. Pour onto a plate to cool. Coarsely chop and set aside.

MAKE THE VINAIGRETTE. In a small bowl, whisk together the vinegar, sugar, poppy seeds, dry mustard, and a pinch each of salt and pepper. Add the oil in a thin stream, whisking constantly until the dressing is well blended.

MAKE THE SALAD. In a large bowl, toss together the spinach, strawberries, and pecans. Add half of the vinaigrette, and toss gently to coat. Add more vinaigrette as needed (you may not need all of it). Top with the cheese.

Makes 6 servings

¼ cup pecans

FOR THE POPPY SEED VINAIGRETTE

¼ cup white wine vinegar

2 tablespoons sugar

2 teaspoons poppy seeds

½ teaspoon dry mustard

Salt and and pepper

¾ cup canola oil

FOR THE SALAD

6 cups baby spinach leaves

2 cups strawberries, hulled and halved

½ cup crumbled goat cheese or feta cheese

Main Dishes

Pesto Pasta

ASK FOR HELP!

You may not need all of the pesto for your pasta. If you have any left over, stir it into a little mayonnaise to spread on a sandwich (it's great on BLTs!), swirl into a bowl of vegetable or chicken noodle soup, spread it on pizza, or drizzle it over eggs.

COOK THE PASTA. Cook the pasta following the package directions. Before draining, carefully scoop out about ½ cup of the cooking water and set it aside.

MAKE THE PESTO. Meanwhile, in a blender or a food processor, coarsely chop the nuts and garlic together. Add the 2 cups basil and the oil, and process until the mixture forms a coarse paste. Add the ½ cup cheese and process just enough to mix everything together. The pesto should be fairly smooth but still have some texture. Season with salt.

MAKE THE PASTA. Put the cooked pasta in a large, shallow bowl. Add a large scoop of the pesto (don't add all of it—you may not need it). Add a few tablespoons of the pasta cooking water to thin the sauce a bit. Toss well. The pesto should be creamy and coat the pasta without too much extra. Add more pesto, if you like, and toss again. To serve, top with additional Parmesan cheese and basil leaves.

Makes 4 servings

1 lb gemelli or fusilli pasta

¼ cup pine nuts

¼ cup walnuts

1 clove garlic

2 cups loosely packed fresh basil leaves, plus more for garnish

½ cup olive oil

½ cup grated Parmesan cheese, plus more for garnish

Salt

COOKING TIP!
To store leftover pesto, transfer it to a bowl, smooth the surface, cover with a thin layer of olive oil, cover with plastic wrap or a lid, and refrigerate; it will keep for 2–3 days.

ASK FOR HELP!

Spring Stir-Fry with Veggies & Shrimp

This dish gets its name from its star vegetables—both peas and asparagus are in season in the spring, which means they're some of the first vegetables to be ready for harvest from the garden. (But of course you can make this any time of year—or try it with green beans, zucchini, or sugar snap peas.) The bottoms of the asparagus stalks are tough and not fun to eat. Just bend them toward the end, and they will snap off.

COOK THE VEGGIES. Put the oil in a wok or large frying pan with a lid. Set the wok over medium-high heat. Add the garlic and ginger, and cook, stirring constantly, until the garlic is fragrant, about 30 seconds. Add the peas and asparagus, and stir to coat with oil. Cook, stirring often, for 1 minute.

COOK THE SHRIMP. Sprinkle 3 tablespoons water in the pan. Cover and cook just until the vegetables are bright green, 1–2 minutes. Add the shrimp and cook, uncovered, stirring often, until they are starting to turn pink and firm up, 2–3 minutes more. Add the broth and soy sauce and bring to a simmer, then immediately remove from the heat.

SERVE THE STIR-FRY. Serve with the rice on the side.

Makes 4 servings

1 tablespoon canola oil

2 cloves garlic, minced or pushed through a garlic press

1 (1-inch) piece fresh ginger, peeled and grated or minced

1 cup fresh or frozen peas

¾ lb thin asparagus, stem ends removed, spears cut diagonally into 1¼-inch pieces

¾ lb medium shrimp, peeled and deveined

⅓ cup chicken broth or vegetable broth

1 tablespoon soy sauce

2 cups cooked white rice

Sweet Potato Tacos with Black Beans, Corn & Avocado

Who says tacos have to be chicken or beef? These veggie-stuffed tacos are colorful, healthy, and delicious. You won't miss the meat!

BAKE THE SWEET POTATO. Preheat the oven to 425°F. Pile the sweet potato cubes in the center of a rimmed baking sheet. Drizzle with 2 tablespoons of the oil and toss to coat evenly. Sprinkle with the chili powder, and season with salt and pepper; toss again. Spread the sweet potato in a single layer. Bake, stirring once halfway through baking time, until tender, about 15 minutes.

WARM THE TORTILLAS. Wrap the tortillas in aluminum foil, and place in the oven about 5 minutes before the sweet potato is ready. After the sweet potato is removed, turn the oven off and leave the tortillas in the oven to stay warm until ready to use.

PREPARE THE BEANS. Meanwhile, in a frying pan over medium heat, warm the remaining 1 tablespoon oil. Add the onion and cook, stirring occasionally, until tender, about 5 minutes. Add the garlic and cook, stirring often, for 1 minute longer. Stir in the cumin and coriander, then add the beans and stir until heated through, 1–2 minutes.

ASSEMBLE & SERVE THE TACOS. Place 2 warmed tortillas on each of 4 plates. Top each tortilla with one-eighth each of the sweet potato, beans, corn, avocado, cheese, and cilantro. Finish with a squeeze of lime juice. Fold the tortillas in half.

Makes about 4 servings

1 large sweet potato (about 1¼ lb), peeled and cut into ½-inch cubes

3 tablespoons olive oil

Big pinch of chili powder

Salt and pepper

8 corn tortillas (8 inch)

½ small yellow onion, finely chopped

1 clove garlic, minced

½ teaspoon ground cumin

¼ teaspoon ground coriander

1 can (14 oz) black beans, drained and rinsed

¾ cup frozen corn, thawed and drained

½ avocado, peeled and cut into 8 slices

½ cup crumbled feta cheese

½ cup chopped fresh cilantro leaves

2 limes, halved

Chicken & Coconut Curry

ASK FOR HELP!

This curry gets a big punch of flavor from a magic ingredient: Thai-style curry paste. There are three different kinds of curry paste—red, yellow, and green. This recipe calls for green because it's the mildest. If you like your food spicy, feel free to try one of the other types.

BOIL THE POTATO. Bring a large pot of salted water to boiling over high heat. Add the sweet potato and cook until fork-tender, about 6 minutes. Drain, transfer to a large bowl, and set aside.

COOK THE CHICKEN. In a large, heavy-bottom saucepan, heat 1 tablespoon of the oil over medium-high heat. Season the chicken all over with salt and pepper. Add it to the hot oil and cook, stirring a few times, until browned on all sides, about 4 minutes total. Using a slotted spoon, transfer to a plate and set aside.

COOK THE VEGGIES. Add the remaining 1 tablespoon oil to the same pan. Add the onion and bell pepper, season with salt and pepper, and cook, stirring, until the vegetables are soft, about 4 minutes. Stir in the garlic and ginger, and cook, stirring, for 2 minutes. Transfer the onion–bell pepper mixture to the bowl with the sweet potatoes.

Makes 6 servings

1 large sweet potato (about 1¼ lb), peeled and cut into ½-inch cubes

2 tablespoons canola oil

1 lb boneless, skinless chicken thighs, cut into 1-inch pieces

Salt and pepper

1 yellow onion, cut into 1-inch pieces

1 red bell pepper, seeded and cut into 1-inch pieces

3 cloves garlic, minced

1 (2-inch) piece fresh ginger, peeled and grated or minced

1 can (14 oz) coconut milk

2 tablespoons green curry paste

1 cup chicken broth

2 tablespoons fish sauce

4 fresh basil leaves, torn

3 cups cooked rice

MAKE THE CURRY. Open the coconut milk can, but don't shake it before opening. Spoon out the thick cream from the top of the can and add it to the saucepan along with the green curry paste; stir to combine. Whisk in the rest of the coconut milk, the broth, and the fish sauce, and bring to a simmer over medium-high heat. Return the chicken to the pan. Add the sweet potatoes and other vegetables to the pan, and simmer until chicken is cooked through and vegetables are warm, about 5 minutes. Stir in the basil, and serve with rice.

Spaghetti Squash Pizza Bowls

When it's baked, the inside of spaghetti squash turns into sunny yellow strands that look like spaghetti, with a nutty, slightly sweet flavor—perfect for tossing with marinara sauce and topping with melted cheese.

PREPARE & PREHEAT. Preheat the oven to 400°F. Line a large rimmed baking sheet with parchment paper.

CUT THE SQUASHES IN HALF. Ask an adult for help with this step. On a cutting board, use a large, sharp knife to cut off about 1 inch from both ends of each squash. Stand 1 squash upright on the cutting board, and carefully cut the squash in half lengthwise. Scoop out and discard the seeds and fibers. Repeat with the second squash. Drizzle the cut surface of each half with 1 tablespoon of the oil, then sprinkle with salt and pepper. Place the halves, cut side down, on the prepared baking sheet.

BAKE THE SQUASH HALVES. Bake the squash until the flesh is golden brown and easily pierced with a fork, 45–50 minutes. Let cool on the pan on a wire rack until cool enough to handle, 10–15 minutes. Then using a fork and starting at one end of a squash half, scrape the flesh lengthwise into a large bowl to create strands that look like spaghetti. Repeat with the remaining halves.

FINISH THE BOWLS. Add the 1 cup Parmesan cheese and the marinara to the squash, and toss to combine. Season with salt and pepper, and toss again. Divide the squash into four equal piles on the parchment-lined baking sheet. Top each pile with ½ cup of the mozzarella. Return the baking sheet to the oven, and bake until the cheese is melted and starting to brown, 15–20 minutes.

SERVE THE BOWLS. Using a large spoon or spatula, transfer each pile of cheese-topped squash to an individual serving bowl. Sprinkle with more Parmesan cheese and the basil (if using).

Makes 4 servings

2 spaghetti squash (about 3 lb each)

4 tablespoons olive oil

Salt and pepper

1 cup grated Parmesan cheese, plus more for serving

2 cups marinara sauce

2 cups shredded mozzarella cheese

Fresh basil leaves, for serving (optional)

Steamed Salmon with Asparagus & Bell Pepper

Salmon and vegetables are drizzled with a slightly sweet soy-sesame sauce before they're sealed up in individual foil packets and baked in the oven. Opening a packet is like opening a dinnertime present—and it smells so good! You could serve this with hot cooked rice on the side, but it's delicious as is too.

MAKE THE SAUCE. Preheat the oven to 450°F. Cut 4 sheets of aluminum foil each about 18 inches long. In a blender, combine the lime juice, soy sauce, sugar, sesame oil, ginger, garlic, and red pepper flakes, and blend until smooth.

ASSEMBLE THE FISH PACKETS. Place 1 foil sheet on a work surface. Place a salmon fillet on one half of the foil. Mound one-fourth each of the asparagus and bell pepper on top of the salmon, and top with one-fourth of the green onions. Drizzle with about 2 tablespoons of the sauce. Fold the uncovered half of the foil over the salmon, and tightly roll up the edges together on 3 sides to seal. Place the packet on a large rimmed baking sheet. Repeat with the remaining ingredients to assemble 3 more packets.

BAKE & SERVE THE FISH & VEGGIES. Bake the packets for 10 minutes. Remove from the oven and let cool slightly. Carefully open the packets to release the steam. Transfer the salmon and vegetables to 4 individual plates.

Makes 4 servings

2 tablespoons fresh lime juice

1 tablespoon plus 1 teaspoon soy sauce

1 tablespoon firmly packed light brown sugar

1 tablespoon toasted sesame oil

1 (1-inch) piece fresh ginger, peeled and roughly chopped

1 clove garlic

Pinch of red pepper flakes

4 salmon fillets (about 6 oz each)

¼ lb asparagus, stem ends removed, spears cut diagonally into 2-inch pieces

1 red bell pepper, seeded and thinly sliced

6 green onions, thinly sliced

Cheddar, Pear & Prosciutto Panini

This is really just a fancy version of a grilled ham and cheese sandwich. The "ham" is prosciutto (pronounced "pruh-SHOO-tow")—a kind of Italian ham that comes in very thin slices—and the cheese is a tangy white cheddar. The pear slices add a little sweetness that is delicious with the salty ham and cheese.

CUT THE PEARS. Stand the pears upright on a cutting board and, using a sharp knife, very carefully cut them lengthwise into thin slices, stopping to turn the pear when you hit the core.

ASSEMBLE THE SANDWICHES. Lay the bagel bottoms on the counter, and top each with 1 slice of the cheese. Divide the prosciutto and pear slices evenly over the cheese, then top each stack with another slice of cheese. Spread the cut side of the bagel tops with the pesto (if using) and place them, pesto side down, over the cheese on each sandwich. Spread the top and bottom of each sandwich with ½ tablespoon of the butter.

GRILL THE SANDWICHES. Heat a frying pan over medium heat. Add the sandwiches. Place a flat, heavy lid or heatproof plate on the sandwiches to press them down. Cook the sandwiches, turning once (replacing the weight), until golden brown on both sides and cheese is melted, about 4 minutes total. Cut each sandwich in half.

Makes 2 servings

2 firm pears

2 everything bagels or brioche buns, halved

4 thin slices white cheddar cheese

4 slices prosciutto or cooked bacon, halved crosswise

2 tablespoons store-bought pesto (optional)

2 tablespoons butter, at room temperature

Fresh Tomato Tart

ASK FOR HELP!

Puff pastry—which you'll find in the freezer section of your grocery store near the pies and piecrusts—is so much fun. As it bakes, it puffs up into lots of flaky, crispy, buttery layers. Assembling this tart is like painting a picture—and in the end, you get to eat it!

PREPARE & PREHEAT. Preheat the oven to 425°F. Line a rimmed baking sheet with parchment paper.

ROLL OUT THE DOUGH. Lightly sprinkle a clean countertop with flour. Lay the puff pastry on the counter and very carefully unfold it. Lightly sprinkle the top with flour. Using a rolling pin, roll out the pastry to an 11 x 11-inch square. Carefully place the square on the prepared baking sheet. Place it in freezer to chill while you prepare the tomatoes.

SLICE THE TOMATOES. Slice the large tomatoes into rounds, and cut the cherry tomatoes in half. Place the tomato slices on a plate and set aside.

BAKE THE PASTRY. Remove the pastry from the freezer. With a sharp knife, cut a 1-inch border along the edges of the puff pastry, being careful not to cut more than halfway through the pastry. Prick the pastry inside of the border all over with a fork. Bake until the pastry is golden brown and flaky, 12–15 minutes. Remove from the oven, and let cool on the baking sheet on a wire rack.

FINISH THE TART AND SERVE. Using a butter knife or the back of a spoon, carefully spread the softened cheese over the pastry. Arrange the tomato slices and cherry tomato halves on top. Sprinkle tomatoes lightly with salt and pepper. Cut tart into pieces.

Makes 6–8 servings

All-purpose flour, for dusting

1 sheet frozen puff pastry, thawed overnight in the refrigerator

3–4 ripe red, orange, or yellow tomatoes, or a combination

8–10 red, orange, or yellow cherry tomatoes, or a combination

1 package (5 oz) soft garlic and herb cheese, at room temperature

Salt and pepper

Tropical Buddha Bowls

What's a Buddha bowl? It's a balanced complete meal made up of grains (like quinoa, rice, or barley), fruits, veggies, greens, and protein (like beans, tofu, chicken, or fish), all served in the same bowl. The "tropical" ingredients in this Buddha bowl are the mango, coconut, and macadamia nuts.

PREPARE THE QUINOA. Cook the quinoa following the package directions. When it's done cooking, cover and keep warm until you are ready to serve.

MAKE THE VINAIGRETTE. While the quinoa is cooking, make the vinaigrette. In a jar with a lid, combine the oil, lime juice, vinegar, water, and sugar. Place the lid on top, secure tightly, and shake well until evenly mixed. Season with salt and pepper, and set aside.

CUT THE MANGO & AVOCADO. Hold the mango upright on a cutting board. Using a large, sharp knife, cut down through the mango, top to bottom, just to one side of the center to cut the mango flesh from the pit. Repeat on the other side. Using a small, sharp knife, cut off the mango peel, dice or slice the flesh, and set aside. Using the small knife, cut into the center of the avocado, cutting all the way around the avocado when you reach the big round pit in the center. Separate the avocado halves. Use the tip of a spoon to remove the pit, then remove the peel, and dice or slice the avocado. Set aside.

ASSEMBLE THE BOWLS. Divide the quinoa evenly among 4 bowls. Place the kale in a medium bowl. Shake the vinaigrette again, then drizzle 1 tablespoon of the vinaigrette over the kale and toss to mix. Arrange the kale over the quinoa. Arrange the mango, avocado, chicken (if using), coconut, and cilantro on top, dividing each ingredient evenly. Sprinkle the macadamia nuts evenly over the top. Pass the remaining vinaigrette at the table.

Makes 4 servings

1 cup dry quinoa

FOR THE VINAIGRETTE

¼ cup olive oil

1 tablespoon fresh lime juice

1 tablespoon white wine vinegar

1 tablespoon water

¼ teaspoon sugar

Salt and pepper

FOR THE TOPPINGS

2 cups loosely packed baby kale or mixed salad greens

1 mango, pitted, peeled, and sliced

1 avocado, halved, pitted, peeled, and sliced

1 cup diced cooked chicken (optional)

½ cup toasted coconut chips (Tip, page 25)

¼ cup fresh cilantro leaves

½ cup chopped macadamia nuts

ASK FOR HELP!

Ginger-Soy Glazed Chicken Thighs

These chicken thighs are super flavorful, thanks to a soak in a gingery, garlicky marinade. Marinate them anywhere from 30 minutes to up to 1 day—the longer they soak, the more flavor they will have. After the chicken is cooked, the marinade is boiled to make a deliciously sweet and sticky glaze. Because it had raw chicken in it, be sure to let it boil for at least 1 minute to make it safe to eat. Stir-fried snow peas are a perfect side!

MAKE THE MARINADE. In a shallow glass or ceramic dish, combine the sugar, soy sauce, ginger, garlic, and 1 teaspoon of the oil. Stir until blended and the sugar dissolves. Add the chicken thighs and stir to coat. Cover and let marinate in the refrigerator for at least 30 minutes or up to 1 day.

COOK THE CHICKEN. In a frying pan, heat the remaining 1 teaspoon oil over medium heat. Remove the chicken thighs from the marinade, reserving the marinade, and add them to the pan. Cook, turning once, until browned and cooked through, 10–12 minutes total. Watch carefully and turn down the heat if the glaze starts to burn. Transfer the thighs to a plate.

MAKE THE GLAZE. Pour the reserved marinade into the frying pan and boil until reduced to a glaze, about 1–2 minutes; do not burn. Remove the pan from the heat, add the chicken thighs, and turn to coat with the glaze. Transfer to dinner plates, and sprinkle with sesame seeds.

Makes 2–4 servings

FOR THE MARINADE

¼ cup light brown sugar

3 tablespoons soy sauce

1 tablespoon minced fresh ginger

2 cloves garlic, minced

2 teaspoons canola oil

FOR THE CHICKEN

4 boneless, skinless chicken thighs (about 1¼ lb total weight)

Sesame seeds, for garnish

Sweet Treats

No-Bake Cheesecake Jars

When Barbie has friends over for a nice dinner, she likes to make these individual cheesecakes for dessert. They can be made up to 2 days ahead of time, which means she has one less thing to make the day of the dinner—and they can be topped with pretty much anything you like. Fresh fruit is always good, but you can also substitute or add your favorite jam, chocolate syrup, a caramel drizzle, or toasted sliced almonds, chopped pecans, or coconut.

MAKE THE CRUST. In a small bowl, combine the graham cracker crumbs, butter, and the 2 tablespoons sugar, and stir until blended. Divide the mixture among 5 half-pint jars or 12-oz glasses, then use the handle end of a wooden spoon to pack down the crumbs. Refrigerate until firm, 10–15 minutes.

MAKE THE CHEESECAKE. Meanwhile, in a large bowl, beat the cream cheese and the remaining ⅓ cup sugar with an electric mixer on medium speed or by hand until smooth. Beat in ¼ cup of the cream, the lemon juice, and the vanilla.

MICROWAVE THE GELATIN. Put the water in a microwave-safe bowl. Sprinkle the gelatin over the surface and let soften for 2 minutes. Microwave on high until the gelatin dissolves, about 5 seconds. Remove from the microwave, and stir in the remaining ¼ cup cream. Add the gelatin mixture to the cream cheese mixture and beat until fluffy, about 1 minute with an electric mixer on medium speed or 3 minutes by hand. Spoon the filling into the jars, dividing it evenly. Cover and refrigerate until firm, at least 1 hour or up to 2 days. Divide the fruit evenly among the jars before serving.

Makes 5 servings

¾ cup graham cracker crumbs (from about 6 graham crackers)

2 tablespoons butter, melted

2 tablespoons plus ⅓ cup sugar

1 lb cream cheese, at room temperature

½ cup heavy cream

1 tablespoon fresh lemon juice

½ teaspoon vanilla extract

1 tablespoon water

½ teaspoon unflavored gelatin

1 cup fresh raspberries, blueberries, sliced strawberries, halved blackberries, pitted halved cherries, or diced fresh peaches

Dressed-Up Box Brownies

ASK FOR HELP!

Brownies made from a box are delicious and great to try if you're a beginner baker. That doesn't mean they're boring, though! Fancy them up with one of these yummy versions. Be sure to include the extra ingredients you'll need on your grocery list.

PREPARE & PREHEAT. Preheat the oven to 350°F. Butter a 9 x 13-inch baking pan.

MAKE THE BROWNIES. Make the brownie batter following the package directions. Pour it into the buttered pan, and follow the directions below for the version you would like to make.

Makes 12 servings

Butter for greasing

1 box (about 22 oz) brownie mix (for a 9 x 13-inch pan)

Eggs

Vegetable oil

S'MORE: Make the brownie batter and bake as directed. About 10–12 minutes before the end of baking, crush 6 graham crackers with your hands and scatter evenly over the top. Place 12 jumbo marshmallows over the graham crackers, spacing them evenly. Continue baking until the marshmallows are golden brown, 10–14 minutes.

PEPPERMINT CRUNCH: Make the brownie batter as directed, but mix in 2 teaspoons peppermint extract. Bake as directed. Meanwhile, put 1 cup unwrapped hard peppermint candies in a large heavy-duty zip-top plastic bag. Seal the bag and, using a meat pounder or hammer, crush the candies into small pieces. About 10–12 minutes before the end of baking, sprinkle the crushed candies evenly over the brownie batter. Continue baking as directed.

BLACK BOTTOM: In a small bowl, whisk 8 oz softened cream cheese, 1 large egg, ⅓ cup sugar, and ½ teaspoon vanilla extract until blended; set aside. Make the brownie batter as directed. Scrape the batter into the prepared pan and spread evenly. Spoon the cream cheese mixture over the top. Using a chopstick or knife, gently swirl the brownie and cream cheese batters together in a series of figure eights. Bake as directed.

Dark Chocolate–Banana Milkshakes

ASK FOR HELP!

These creamy, cold, and chocolaty milkshakes will hit the spot on a hot day! Make it a malt with a couple spoonfuls of malted milk powder, if you like.

BLEND THE INGREDIENTS. In a blender, combine bananas, ice cream, chocolate syrup, and ¼ cup milk. Blend until smooth, adding more milk if necessary.

SERVE THE MILKSHAKES. Pour the milkshake into chilled tall glasses, and garnish each shake with a dollop of whipped cream (if using).

Makes 4 servings

2 bananas, peeled, sliced, and frozen

1 pint dark chocolate ice cream

¼ cup chocolate syrup

¼ cup whole milk, plus more if needed

Whipped cream (optional)

Oatmeal-Raisin Cookies

 ASK FOR HELP!

If there's such a thing as comfort-food cookies, these cinnamon-spiced treats are it. There's a reason they've been a go-to treat for nearly forever—and always will be. They're best with a glass of cold milk, of course!

MIX THE DRY INGREDIENTS. Preheat the oven to 350°F. Line 2 baking sheets with parchment paper. In a bowl, stir together the flour, baking powder, cinnamon, and salt. Set aside.

BLEND THE BUTTER & SUGAR. In the bowl of an electric mixer, combine the butter and sugars. Beat on low speed until combined, then raise the speed to medium and beat until light and fluffy, about 3 minutes.

COMBINE THE INGREDIENTS. Using a rubber spatula, scrape the butter mixture down the sides of the bowl. Add the eggs, one at a time, beating well after adding each one. Add the vanilla and beat to combine. Reduce the speed to low, and slowly add the flour mixture and the rolled oats, beating just until combined. Use a wooden spoon or sturdy spatula to fold in the raisins until they are evenly distributed.

BAKE THE COOKIES. Using a large spoon, scoop round, heaping tablespoons of dough and place them 3 inches apart on the baking sheets. Bake until lightly browned, 15–20 minutes. Let the cookies cool on the pans for 5 minutes, then transfer to wire racks and let cool completely.

Makes about 24 cookies

1½ cups all-purpose flour

1 teaspoon baking powder

1 tablespoon ground cinnamon

¼ teaspoon salt

½ cup unsalted butter, at room temperature

1 cup firmly packed dark brown sugar

½ cup granulated sugar

2 large eggs

2 teaspoons vanilla extract

1½ cups old-fashioned rolled oats

2 cups raisins

Gluten-Free Almond Cake

Even if you don't have to be gluten-free, this moist, nutty-flavored cake is a real treat! To be sure it comes out of the pan easily, line it with parchment paper. Just set the pan on a piece of parchment, trace around it with a pencil, and cut it out.

PREPARE THE PAN. Preheat the oven to 350°F. Grease a 9-inch cake pan with butter, line the bottom with parchment paper, and grease the paper.

BEAT THE EGG YOLKS & SUGAR. Separate the eggs, putting the whites in one bowl and the yolks in another bowl. (The easiest way to separate an egg is to gently crack it on the edge of a bowl, then let the whites drip into it. When only the yolk is left, pour it into another bowl.) Add the ¾ cup granulated sugar to the yolks, and beat with an electric mixer until pale yellow and creamy. Beat in the lemon zest and almond extract, then stir in the almond meal. Set aside.

COAT THE ALMONDS. Scoop 1 teaspoon of the egg whites and 1 teaspoon of the granulated sugar into a small bowl and beat with a fork until frothy. Add the almonds, toss to coat with the egg white mixture, and set aside.

BEAT THE REMAINING EGG WHITES. Using clean beaters, beat the remaining egg whites until foamy, then beat in the remaining 1 teaspoon granulated sugar and continue beating until stiff peaks form. Using a rubber spatula, stir one-quarter of the whipped egg whites into the yolk mixture to lighten it, then gently fold in the remaining egg whites in two batches. Pour the cake batter into the prepared pan.

BAKE THE CAKE. Bake for 20 minutes. Sprinkle the almonds evenly over the top and continue to bake until the cake is deep golden brown and pulls away from sides of the pan, 10–12 minutes longer. Let cool in the pan for 10 minutes, then carefully remove the cake from the pan. Transfer to a wire rack and let cool completely. To serve, cut into wedges and top with strawberries (if using).

Makes 6–8 servings

Butter, for greasing

4 large eggs, at room temperature

¾ cup plus 2 teaspoons granulated sugar

¼ teaspoon finely grated lemon peel

½ teaspoon almond or vanilla extract

1 cup almond meal

½ cup sliced almonds

Sliced fresh strawberries, for serving (optional)

Chunky Applesauce

To mix it up, you can use 2 pears and 2 apples, or all pears. You can also stir in a sprinkle of cinnamon, if you like. This is nice by itself, over ice cream, or on top of pancakes.

CUT THE APPLES. Peel the apples and cut into quarters. Using a small, sharp knife, cut out the cores. Cut the apple quarters into chunks. You should have about 4 cups diced apples.

COOK THE APPLES. Place the apples in a saucepan and add the sugar, water, lemon juice, and a pinch of salt. Stir well. Set the pan over medium-high heat and bring to a boil. Reduce the heat to low, cover, and simmer until tender, about 30 minutes. If the apples begin to dry out before they are soft, add a little more water.

MASH THE APPLES. Uncover the pan, and mash the apples lightly with a wooden spoon or a rubber spatula. Continue to cook for 5 minutes longer to evaporate some of the excess moisture. The applesauce should be thick. Remove from the heat, and serve warm or chilled. Store leftovers in an airtight container in the refrigerator for up to 3 days.

Makes 4 servings

4 Fuji or Braeburn apples

¼ cup sugar

¼ cup water

2 teaspoons fresh lemon juice

Salt

Raspberry Swirl Frozen Yogurt Pops

When it's hot outside, cool down with these healthy treats. This recipe makes 4 pops, but if you have an ice-pop mold with 8 cavities, just double all of the ingredients. You can also substitute frozen strawberries or blueberries for the raspberries, if you like.

MASH THE BERRIES. In a small bowl, mash the raspberries with the powdered sugar. In another bowl, combine the yogurt, honey, and vanilla, and stir until the mixture is smooth.

FILL THE MOLDS. Using an ice-pop mold with four 4-fl oz cavities, spoon 2 generous tablespoons of the yogurt mixture into the bottom of each cavity. Add 2 teaspoons of the raspberry mixture. Do this layering twice more.

FREEZE THE POPS. To create raspberry swirls and streaks, work a thin-blade knife up and down and twist it in the yogurt. Top off each cavity with the remaining yogurt. Insert a wooden stick into each pop, leaving about 2 inches sticking up. Freeze the pops until solid, about 4 hours.

UNMOLD THE POPS. To unmold, fill a large bowl with hot tap water. Hold the mold in the water for 1 minute. Run the blade of a small knife around the inside between the mold and the yogurt. Using a gentle rocking motion, slowly and firmly pull to release the pops from the mold. Repeat dipping the mold in the hot water, if necessary. Serve right away.

Makes 4 servings

½ cup frozen unsweetened raspberries, partially thawed

2 tablespoons powdered sugar

1½ cups plain whole milk Greek yogurt

3 tablespoons honey

½ teaspoon vanilla extract

4 (4-inch) ice-pop molds

4 wooden ice-pop sticks

Pear Handpies

The name says it all—a handpie is a cute little pocket pie you can eat with your hands. If you like, you can swap a medium apple for the pear to make apple handpies.

PREPARE THE PASTRY & FILLING. Preheat the oven to 375°F. Line a rimmed baking sheet with parchment paper. Place the pear in a bowl, sprinkle with the lemon juice, and toss to coat. Add the 2 tablespoons sugar, the 2 teaspoons flour, the cinnamon, and nutmeg. Stir gently until evenly mixed.

ASSEMBLE THE PIES. Lightly dust the counter with flour. Using a rolling pin, very lightly roll out the piecrust and cut into four 5-inch rounds. Spoon one-fourth of the pear mixture over half of each dough round, keeping a 1-inch border around the edges uncovered. Beat the egg and milk together. Using a pastry brush, lightly brush the egg mixture around the edges of the dough rounds. Fold the dough over the filling, and press the tines of a fork along the seam to seal. Place the pies on the prepared baking sheet.

BAKE THE PIES. Brush the top of each pie with the egg mixture, then sprinkle with a little sugar. Cut a few small slits in the top of each pie. Bake until golden brown, 12–20 minutes. Let cool on a wire rack. Serve warm or at room temperature.

Makes 4 servings

1 pear, peeled and finely chopped

1 teaspoon fresh lemon juice

2 tablespoons sugar, plus more for sprinkling

2 teaspoons all-purpose flour, plus more for dusting

¼ teaspoon ground cinnamon

⅛ teaspoon ground nutmeg

1 store-bought piecrust for a single-crust pie

1 large egg

1 tablespoon milk

Fruit Salad with Honey & Mint

This stone fruit and melon salad is a light and refreshing dessert, delicious topped with a dollop of whipped cream, ice cream, or yogurt. You can also serve it as a side dish for breakfast or brunch.

MAKE THE DRESSING. In a small bowl, stir together the honey, mint, and lime peel.

MAKE THE SALAD. In a large serving bowl, combine the peaches, nectarines, melon, and grapes. Drizzle the fruit with the lime juice and stir gently to coat. Drizzle with the dressing, turn the fruit once or twice to coat evenly, and serve.

Makes 4–6 servings

FOR THE DRESSING

¼ cup honey

2 tablespoons minced fresh mint

2 teaspoons finely grated lime peel

FOR THE SALAD

2 ripe peaches, pitted and cut into ½-inch-thick slices

2 ripe nectarines, pitted and cut into ½-inch-thick slices

½ cantaloupe or other melon, seeded, peeled, and cut into ½-inch cubes

1 cup seedless grapes, halved

Juice of 1 lime

Chewy Chocolate Meringues

These cloud-like cookies are crisp on the outside and delightfully chewy on the inside. Whipping the egg whites causes tiny air bubbles to form. The heat from the oven makes the bubbles expand, puffing the meringues as they bake.

PREPARE THE OVEN. Space 2 racks evenly in the middle of the oven and preheat to 350°F. Line 2 rimmed baking sheets with parchment paper.

SIMMER THE EGG WHITES & SUGAR. In a metal or glass bowl that will sit on top of a saucepan, whisk together the egg whites and sugar. Add about 2 inches of water to the saucepan and bring it to a boil. Reduce heat to low so the water just simmers. Set the bowl of egg whites over (not touching) the water in the saucepan, and whisk constantly until the sugar is completely dissolved. Remove from the heat.

BEAT THE EGG WHITES. Using a stand mixer fitted with the whisk attachment, beat the egg white mixture on high speed until stiff and glossy. Using a fine-mesh sieve or a flour sifter, sift the cocoa over the meringue. Sprinkle with the chocolate, then gently fold together with a rubber spatula until combined.

BAKE THE MERINGUES. Drop the meringue mixture by heaping tablespoonfuls, spaced slightly apart, onto the prepared baking sheets. Bake for 9 minutes. Rotate the pans between racks, and bake until the cookies are fluffy, full of cracks, and spring back when touched, about 9 minutes more. Carefully pick up the parchment sheets and transfer the cookies, keeping the cookies on the parchment, to wire racks to cool.

Makes about 12 servings

7 large egg whites

1¾ cups sugar

5 tablespoons unsweetened natural cocoa powder

4 oz bittersweet chocolate, finely chopped

ASK FOR HELP!

Pluot Galette

The name of this recipe may sound super fancy—and this is a perfect dessert for a special occasion—but a galette is really just a French tart that isn't made in a pan, so it can be loose and casual looking (in fact, it's supposed to be!). As for the pluots— those are simply a cross between plums and apricots. If you can't find them, you can substitute either fruit.

ROLL OUT THE DOUGH. Dust the counter with a little flour. Roll out the piecrust into a 12-inch round that is about ⅛ inch thick. Line a rimmed baking sheet with parchment paper. Carefully transfer the dough round to the baking sheet.

FILL THE GALETTE. In a large bowl, toss the pluot slices with 3 tablespoons of the sugar. Pour the filling into the center of the dough and spread evenly, leaving a 2-inch border of dough uncovered along the edge. Fold the edge of the dough up and over the pluots, loosely pleating as you go and leaving the fruit uncovered in the center. Refrigerate until the dough is firm, at least 30 minutes.

BAKE THE GALETTE. Preheat the oven to 400°F. Whisk the egg yolk with 1 teaspoon water. Brush the dough with the egg mixture, and sprinkle with the remaining 1 tablespoon sugar. Bake the galette until the crust is golden brown and the pluots are tender, 45–60 minutes. The last 20 minutes of baking, cover the tart loosley with foil to keep it from burning. Let cool for at least 20 minutes before serving. Garnish with pistachios and mint (if using).

Makes 6–8 servings

All-purpose flour

1 store-bought piecrust for a single-crust pie

1½ lb pluots, thinly sliced

4 tablespoons sugar

1 egg yolk

Chopped pistachios, for garnish (optional)

Fresh mint leaves, for garnish (optional)

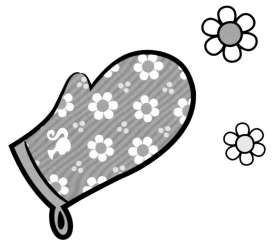

Sautéed Bananas with Yogurt & Honey

ASK FOR HELP!

To make this recipe, you want bananas that aren't too ripe or too green. If they're too ripe, they'll get mushy when you cook them. If they're too green, they won't taste very good. Bananas that are yellow all over with just a few brown speckles are just right.

SAUTÉ THE BANANAS. Heat a frying pan over medium heat until hot but not smoking. Add the butter. Using a spatula, spread the butter evenly over the pan bottom. Add the sliced bananas and cook, stirring occasionally, until browned on both sides, 4–6 minutes.

ASSEMBLE THE DESSERT. Divide the yogurt among individual bowls. Divide the bananas among the bowls, spooning the slices over the yogurt. Drizzle with honey. Serve warm.

Makes 2–4 servings

1 tablespoon unsalted butter

2 large bananas, peeled and sliced

1 cup plain or vanilla Greek-style yogurt

Honey for drizzling

Convert It, Swap It, Halve It

MEASUREMENT CONVERSIONS

3 teaspoons = 1 tablespoon

4 tablespoons = ¼ cup

5 tablespoons plus 1 teaspoon = ⅓ cup

1 cup = 8 fluid ounces

2 cups = 1 pint

2 pints = 1 quart

4 quarts = 1 gallon

4 ounces = ¼ pound

8 ounces = ½ pound

12 ounces = ¾ pound

16 ounces = 1 pound

MISSING SOMETHING?

Buttermilk

For every 1 cup buttermilk needed, stir together 1 cup whole milk and 1 tablespoon fresh lemon juice or distilled white vinegar. Let the mixture sit for a few minutes, or until thickened and slightly curdled.

Heavy Cream

For every 1 cup heavy cream needed, stir together ¾ cup whole milk and ⅓ cup melted and cooled unsalted butter. This substitution will not work if the recipe calls for whipping the cream.

Eggs

For cake and quick bread batters, substitute ¼ cup applesauce or ½ of a mashed banana for every egg called for in the recipe. For cookies, brownies, and muffins, whisk together 1 tablespoon flaxseed meal and 2½ tablespoons water for every egg called for in the recipe. Let stand for 5 minutes, or until thickened, before using. This flaxseed "egg" will not thicken as much as a whisked regular egg.

Index

weldon**owen**

PO Box 3088
San Rafael, CA 94912
www.weldonowen.com

WELDON OWEN INTERNATIONAL
CEO Raoul Goff
Publisher Roger Shaw
Associate Publisher Amy Marr
Editorial Assistant Jourdan Plautz
VP of Creative Chrissy Kwasnik
Design Support Megan Sinead Harris
Managing Editor Katie Killebrew
Production Manager Sam Taylor

Photography Waterbury Publications, Des Moines, IA
Photograph on page 11 by Ted Thomas
Food Stylist Jennifer Peterson

A WELDON OWEN PRODUCTION

Recipes © Weldon Owen International

Printed and bound in China

First printed in 2022
10 9 8 7 6 5 4 3 2 1

Library of Congress Cataloging in
Publication data is available

ISBN: 978-1-68188-833-0

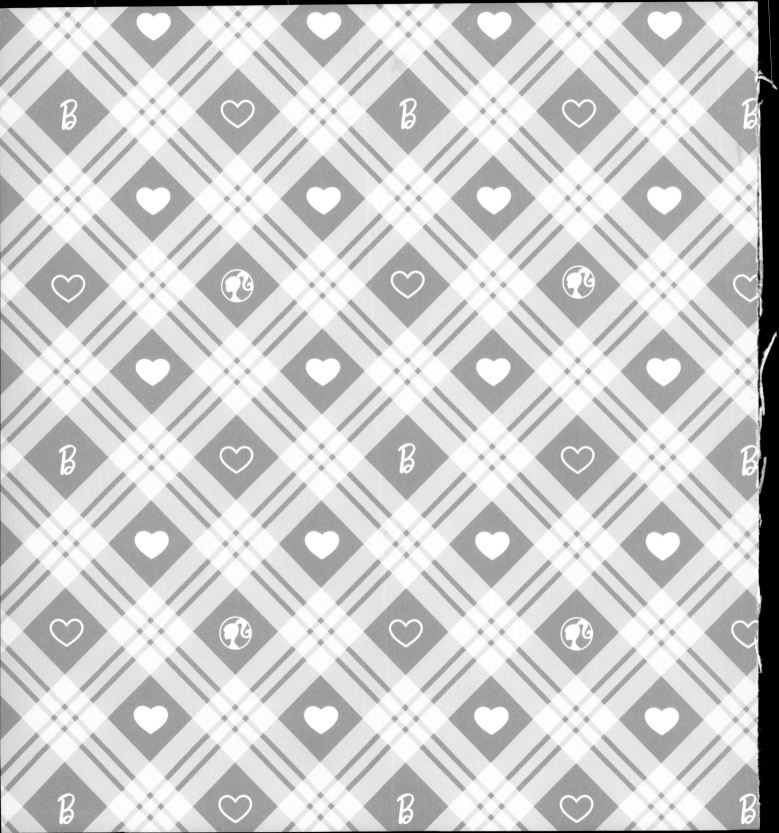